The Trouble with Cats

by Martha Freeman

illustrated by
Cat Bowman
Smith

Holiday House / New York

For Simon, Schuster, Smoke, and Intrepid,
four inspirational cats in one small apartment.
And for the real Holly,
who is not afraid
of anything.

Text copyright © 2000 by Martha Freeman
Illustrations copyright © 2000 Cat Bowman Smith
All Rights Reserved
Printed in the United States of America

Library of Congress Cataloging-in-Publication Data
Freeman, Martha, 1956–
The trouble with cats / by Martha Freeman ; illustrated by Cat Bowman Smith—1st ed.
p. cm.
Summary: After a difficult first week of third grade, Holly begins to adjust
to her new school and living in her new stepfather's tiny apartment
with his four cats.
ISBN 0-8234-1479-5
[1. Schools—Fiction.   2. Stepfathers—Fiction.   3. Cats—Fiction.
4. San Francisco(Calif.)—Fiction.]   I. Smith, Cat Bowman, ill.   II. Title.
Pz7.F87496 Tr 2000
[Fic]—dc21   99-029291

Chapter 1

William has four cats. And every one of them is trouble.

Max Cat always escapes.

George Cat always disappears.

Wilbur Cat eats socks.

And Boo Cat is always somewhere you don't want him to be.

Why did Mom have to marry William? Why did we have to move in with him? And why did he have to have four cats?

I don't like a single one of them. And not a single one of them likes me.

The night before my first day at Market Street School, all four of William's cats slept in my tiny

1

room. Max slept behind my door. George slept under my bed. Wilbur slept in my half-open underwear drawer. And Boo tried to hog my blankets.

In the middle of the night, the cats woke up. They walked across me like I was a lump in the mattress. They swished their tails in my face. They *thumped* and *bumped* and *mrr-r-r-owed.*

I went to the bathroom. When I came back, Boo was sitting in the middle of my pillow, washing his face.

I elbowed Boo onto the floor. But by then I was wide awake. I started worrying all over again about my first day at Market Street School. How mean would the teacher be? How mean would the kids be? What if they thought I was weird? What if the slide was so tall it scared me?

I liked my old school. I liked my old friends, especially Sylvie. I liked the short slide on my old playground.

Boo jumped back on the bed. This time I let him stay.

My mom and dad split up when I was four. After that, Dad moved to L.A. I visit when he's not too busy.

In L.A., there is a car museum with a gold Rolls-Royce. Lots of TV stars live there, too.

But San Francisco, where I live, is better.

San Francisco is the prettiest city in the world. The bay sparkles under a tall, swoopy bridge on one side. The ocean sparkles under a tall, swoopy bridge on the other side. There are skyscrapers and fancy old houses. There are hills so steep you have to breathe hard to climb them.

That's not all that's good. Any old time, you can see people with black lipstick. And rings in their eyebrows. And purple haircuts. Also, there are excellent places to eat ice cream and chocolate and Chinese food.

It is foggy sometimes. But fog lends an air of mystery. That's what William says. He's a boring old lawyer. At night after work, he writes stories. He keeps the stories in a cabinet next to the cat dishes in the laundry room. I started to read one once. The words were long. And it made no sense.

Mom and William got married this summer at San Francisco City Hall. No cake. No flowers. Most important, no flower girl. All I got was a new dress out of a catalog. When it came, it was too big. I looked like I was wearing an old lady's tablecloth.

Chapter 2

On the morning of my first day at Market Street School, one of my socks was missing. I put on the other one and hopped to the kitchen on one foot. Mom was making my favorite breakfast: French toast from sourdough bread.

"I haven't seen your sock, Holly," she answered me. "Maybe Wilbur Cat . . . ?"

Oh, no.

Sure enough, my sock was in Wilbur Cat's dish in the laundry room. I pushed my foot in. My toes came out one end. My heel came out the other.

I wore it anyway. I didn't want to be late.

"Happy first day of third grade!" Mom said when I got to the breakfast table.

I looked down at the French toast. My stomach flopped.

William peeked over the edge of the *San Francisco Chronicle*. "What's the matter, Holly? First-day jitters? Market Street is a fine school. You'll love it."

William thinks saying "You'll love it," means I'll love it. He doesn't understand kids. He was never married until now, so he doesn't have kids of his own. Also, he's forty-eight. That's almost half a century old. He is even bald. For sure, he can't remember being a kid.

Mom squeezed my shoulder. "Do you want strawberry jelly?"

"No, thanks."

Mom looked worried. To make her feel better, I drank my milk. It burbled in my tummy.

William was going to take me to school on his way to his office. It's in a building shaped like a pyramid. Mom works here, in William's tiny apartment. She's an accountant.

"Ready, Holly?" William picked up his briefcase. I picked up my book bag. When William opened the door to the hall, Max Cat escaped.

"Catch him!" William yelled.

But Max had already disappeared up the

stairs. William ran after him. I followed William. But I didn't really care if Max escaped. What I cared about was being late on the first day.

It took William three floors to catch Max. When William came down, he was breathing hard. His face was red.

"*Bad* cat." William handed Max Cat to Mom. I looked at Max's face. He didn't care if he was bad.

Chapter 3

Before Mom married William, we lived in our own house in Noe Valley. It was old. It was falling apart, Mom said. But I didn't care. It was our house.

Mom worked downtown all day. When school got out, I went to A. S. C. in the cafeteria. A. S. C. stands for After-School Club. Sylvie, my best friend, went there, too. We sang songs and played outside and made things with glue and popsicle sticks. Around holidays, we got glitter. For sure, it was babyish. But I liked it because Sylvie was there.

On weekends, Mom and I used to make cookies. Or plant flowers. Or go to the zoo. Or collect sand dollars at Ocean Beach.

Everything changed when Mom met William. Suddenly, he was collecting sand dollars with us. Sometimes, I had to go to Sylvie's house on Saturday. Mom said it was because she and William "needed grown-up time."

What did they do with all that "grown-up time" anyway? Kissy stuff? I, for sure, couldn't picture it.

I liked William okay. Anybody could see he tried to be nice to me. I tried to be nice back. Sometimes he was funny. Like on Easter when he

wore bunny ears. He even stuck a cottonball on his rear end.

When he hopped, the cats freaked out.

William didn't seem like a person who would marry anyone. He seemed like a person who mostly liked cats. So I was for sure surprised when Mom told me the news.

"It will be great for us, too, Holly," she said. "We've decided we'll all live in William's apartment at first. I can quit my job and work from home. No more A.S.C.! You and I will have more time together."

We moved after the wedding. Mom set up her office in what used to be the vacuum cleaner closet. My bedroom used to belong to the cats. William said they would have to learn to share.

And so would I.

Chapter 4

The late bell was ringing when William and I pulled up to Market Street School.

"Do you want me to come in with you?" William asked.

"No!" I answered. "No! I'm okay. Bye." I slammed the car door and ran.

My room was 31. Mom and I had come here on Welcome Back Day to find it and meet my teacher, Mr. Morgan. He seemed okay. But teachers always act okay when moms are around. You can't tell anything from that.

My high-tops' *squish-squisha* sounded loud in the empty hallway. Every other kid was in class already.

When I walked into Room 31, everybody looked. All those eyes froze me. I wanted to escape, like Max. But where would I go? And anyway, what good would it do? Max got caught.

Mr. Morgan didn't see me at first. He was writing on the blackboard.

"Who are *you*?" a blond boy asked. A loud-mouth. The name written on a card in front of him was Jake.

"Don't be a moron," said another boy. "She's Holly. The only one not in her seat." He was a know-it-all. His name card said Zach.

"How come you're late on the first day?" Jake the loudmouth wanted to know. "Nobody's late on the first day."

A couple of people laughed. Mr. Morgan turned and saw me. "There you are."

Had he said it in a mean voice? I couldn't tell.

Then he smiled. "You may put your things over there. Then take your seat at Gold Table. See your name card? I haven't taken roll yet. Class, this is Holly Garland."

Everybody watched me. All those eyes! I was terrified I would burp.

But I made it to my seat. And Mr. Morgan took roll. Then he told us the class rules. And the

13

school rules. And the playground rules. More stuff to worry about. How could I keep so many rules in my head? I knew I would do something wrong. And I might not even mean it.

Chapter 5

My dad in L.A. got married last year. He eloped to Hawaii. "Elope" means I didn't get to be *his* flower girl either. Dad's new wife is named Marcy. She is not as pretty as Mom, if you ask me.

My dad says it's important to "conquer your fears." That means if I'm scared of something, he makes me do it anyway. When I was a first grader, he made me fly home on the airplane by myself. I mean, other passengers were there, and the pilot and all. But there was nobody just with me.

I was so scared I almost threw up the peanuts.

But now I fly by myself all the time. Usually, I ask for two bags of peanuts. I get a whole can of ginger ale, too.

I conquered that fear. So at morning recess, I decided to try the slide. From the ground, it didn't look that tall. I got in line. The loudmouth boy came up behind me: Jake.

"So how come you were late?" Jake asked. "Were you sick or something?"

Then the know-it-all boy came up: Zach. "There's a hole in your right sock," he said.

I bet I turned jelly red. I was going to tell them I was late because Max Cat always tries to escape. And they couldn't blame *me* if Wilbur Cat ate socks. But before I could say anything, it was my turn.

"Hurry up!" said the chubby girl in line behind me.

The slide seemed taller from the top than from the bottom. I could see the towers of the Bay Bridge above the hills.

I took a deep breath. I closed my eyes. I pushed myself away . . . then I grabbed hold and stopped.

"Chicken!" somebody yelled.

I thought about staying up there till the bell rang. When everybody was gone, I could climb down the ladder. Nobody would see. But then I'd be late to class again.

"Hurry up! The bell's going to ring!"

What did I care what they thought anyway? This slide was way too tall. Other kids could risk their lives if they wanted to.

I climbed back down the ladder.

"Baby!"

It was only recess on the first day. And already Market Street School was a disaster.

Chapter 6

Can something be worse than disaster?

Yes.

After lunch, we did math. I got sleepy. It was no surprise. My tummy was full of sloppy joe from the cafeteria. And William's cats had kept me up all night. I put my head down on my desk. Next thing I knew, Mr. Morgan was shaking my shoulder. And everybody was laughing.

I had never been so happy to hear the 3:15 bell ring.

I had to take the bus home. A girl named Kimmi from my class sat down next to me. I felt too shy to say anything. She didn't say anything either.

The bus rumbled up Potrero Street. A sign above the driver said QUIET, PLEASE, and NO GUM! Even so, there was yelling and laughing and gum popping.

"How come you fell asleep?" Kimmi finally asked me.

I was glad for a chance to explain. Maybe Kimmi would understand how William's cats kept me up all night. Then at least she wouldn't think I was weird.

"It was all because of—" I started. But the brakes squeaked, and the doors whooshed open.

"This is my stop," she said. "See ya—bye."

William's apartment is on the third floor. The elevator never works. My book bag weighed a ton by the time I got to the door, 3-C.

Mom was waiting. "I made cookies," she said. "Watch out for Max!"

His stupid little fur face tried to nose out, but I closed the door in time. "You made cookies? I thought you had heaps of work." I threw my book bag into a chair.

"Just a treat for your first day of school. How did it go?" she asked.

I didn't want to say worse than disaster. So I said, "What kind of cookies?"

"Sugar."

"I like chocolate chip." I felt bad as soon as I said it. But I couldn't help it. After everything that had happened, I felt crabby.

Mom refused to be crabby back. "So you're saying you don't want any?" she asked patiently.

"Well . . . I've got math homework. But I guess a couple would be good."

Mom smiled and put cookies on my plate. "So how was it?" She sat down across from me. "Are the kids friendly?"

"They're okay, I guess."

"What did you have for lunch? Do you have homework? Did you play dodgeball at recess? You're good at that. Would you like milk?"

I couldn't answer so many questions at once. "Is it chocolate milk?"

It wasn't. But I took a glass anyway.

"Well?" Mom said.

I sighed. "It's a boring old school with boring old kids. It's just normal. Only the slide's too tall," I added. "It looks *quite* dangerous."

"Is that all that's the matter with school? The slide? Surely, you can get used to that." Mom sounded just like William when he said, "You'll love it."

"When you're done with your snack," Mom went on, "how about helping with the cat count?"

"The what?"

"I know it seems silly," she said, "but William wants me to do a cat count anytime one might be gone. Today I got packages delivered, and Ella—remember my client who makes the dried-fruit pizza? She stopped by, too. You know how Max Cat sneaks out. Not to mention how George Cat disappears. William doesn't want

21

to lose any. They were his whole family—till he got us."

I thought counting cats was a stupid idea. I wished they would *all* disappear. "Do I have to?" I whined.

Mom gave me one of her world-famous, no-nonsense looks. "Yes," she said.

Chapter 7

There is something very spooky about William's cats, if you ask me. They are always in the way unless you want them. Then they are no place at all.

So half an hour later, I was crawling around the apartment, looking for cats to count. And I couldn't find a single one.

"Any luck?" Mom called.

"I thought I was supposed to help *you*." I climbed on the sofa to look at the top shelf of the bookcase. No cats. "But you aren't looking even one bit."

"My job is to check off the cats when you find them," Mom said. "There's a chart on the refrigerator."

Her job didn't sound very big. I was going to

say that. But then I looked under my bed. Two spooky eyes looked back.

"Here's one!" I yelled.

"Which is it?"

"Max."

"Cat One. Check," Mom replied.

Soon I found Boo. He was sharpening his claws on my cowboy hat. When I found Wilbur, he was enjoying his favorite snack. I picked them both up and hauled them to the kitchen. They were big and squirmy in my arms.

"Cat Two and Cat Three." Mom marked them off. "Check and check."

"I'm going to need some new socks, Mom." I dropped the cats and showed her the holes in the one Wilbur just chewed.

"Wear sandals till I have a chance to shop."

"It's foggy out, Mom! My toes will freeze."

"Never mind about that now," she said. "Go find George. I want them all checked off before William gets home."

"Olly olly oxen free!" I called.

But George had disappeared.

Chapter 8

By the time William got home, Mom and I had red knees from crawling on the floor. And there was still no George.

William said we had to keep looking. So for dinner we ate apples and toffee peanuts and barbecue potato chips.

"One time, I found him on the seat of a chair." William pulled each dining room chair out from under the table. No George. "One time he was under the computer cover, asleep on the keyboard. It was rather sweet."

Mom checked the computer. No George.

My knees hurt. I wanted a real dinner. I was

tired of brushing dust bunnies out of my hair. I was crabby.

"There are heaps of cats at the pound, you know," I told William.

"And just what do you mean by that?" he asked.

"Why's this cat so important? Anyway, if he gets hungry, he'll come out. That's what my dad said when Manny disappeared."

"There may be heaps of cats. But there is only one George," William answered. "And who's Manny?"

William opened the refrigerator. Did he expect to find George with the lettuce? No. He got out an Anchor Steam beer.

Mom walked through and explained. "Holly's dad would never let her have a pet. But finally he said all right to a gerbil. That's Manny," she said. "Or rather, that *was* Manny. He got lost and starved. Did you check under the sink?"

"Twice," I said. "And you don't *know* Manny starved. We never found gerbil bones, did we? Maybe he went to a happier home."

At bedtime, we still hadn't found George. I put on my pajamas and brushed my teeth. Then I looked under my bed. Three pairs of spooky eyes looked back.

"I hope you guys don't think you can sleep here all the time," I said. *"Scat! Shoo!"* I flipped the bedspread, but the eyes just stared.

I gave up and sat down on the floor and thought about the next day.

I would stay away from the slide.

I wouldn't eat a sloppy joe.

I would try to explain to Kimmi on the bus.

I did not want to go back to Market Street School. But I would try to conquer my fears.

I got up and pulled the bedspread off my pillow. Something furry scooted away under the covers. For half a second, I thought of Manny. Then I realized it was a cat's tail.

We had worn out our knees looking. And all the time, stupid George Cat was happily asleep.

I threw back the covers. And there was the rest of him. Was that an I'm-sorry look on his face?

No way.

"Cat Four!" I yelled.

There were barefoot thumps in the hall. Then Mom's voice from the kitchen: "Cat Four. Check!"

William came into my room. "Where was the little scamp?"

I nodded at my pillow.

"The old under-the-covers trick, eh, Georgie boy?" William scratched behind George's ears. George arched his back and stretched out his paws. "We were worried about you. Weren't we, Holly?" William asked.

"I'm kind of sleepy now, William," I said.

"Righty-o. See you in the morning. Night, George. Uh, by the way, Holly—do you know where the other cats are?"

"Under the bed."

"Well, isn't that fine? They're learning to share. I knew they would."

Chapter 9

The cats let me sleep that night. I got up early the next morning. I was taking the bus. I couldn't risk cat delays.

I put on my clothes and marched barefoot into the kitchen.

William was sitting at the table reading the *Chronicle*. He looked at his watch. "Seven twenty-five," he said. "Highly impressive."

"Mom?" I felt crabby. But I tried to sound calm.

"Highly impressive," Mom echoed.

So much for being calm. "No, it's not. *I'm* not. Look!" I grabbed my right ankle, held up my foot and wiggled my toes. "What am I supposed to put on this?"

"Oh, dear," Mom said. "I forgot. You mean Wilbur didn't leave even one pair?"

"You ought to remember to close your sock drawer." William turned the page.

"Well, we don't have a lot of choices now," Mom said. "How about if you borrow from me?"

"Your feet are huge!"

Mom looked hurt. "They are *not*. They're quite dainty. Anyway, it's that or frozen toes."

William looked up. "You know what Mark Twain said about San Francisco?" he asked.

I wondered what that had to do with anything. But I said, "No. What?"

"'The coldest winter I ever spent was a summer in San Francisco.'"

Mom laughed.

I didn't.

Mom explained, "William means Mark Twain's toes were cold in September, too."

"Oh." I went to get Mom's socks. The smallest ones I could find were gray. When I put on my sneakers, the socks overflowed. I prayed no kids would see.

The bus comes to the corner at 8:05. At 7:57, I closed William's door and ran down the three

31

flights of stairs. At the bottom, I almost crashed into a grown-up girl with a rainbow mohawk. She was locking the door of 1-C.

"Sorry," I said. "Do you live here? I never saw you."

"Well, now you did." She smiled. "Late as usual. Gotta jet—bye!"

She pushed out the street door ahead of me. The back of her T-shirt said "Moon Glow Dough and Joe." That was the doughnut-and-coffee place down the block.

I was the first one to the stop. But by 8:01, three other kids were waiting with me. One of them was Jake the loudmouth.

"You're the new girl, aren't you? The one who's scared of the slide? What did you get for Problem 2?" he asked me.

I squeezed my eyes shut. I couldn't believe it. I had been so busy looking for George that I forgot the math homework. "Oh, no . . ." I moaned.

"What is it?" Jake wanted to know. "Did your mom make you eat granola for breakfast? My mom does that. Ooooooh," he moaned in a big fake moan. "I know just how you feel."

"It's not granola," I said. "I don't have my homework."

"The first homework?!" Jake couldn't believe it. "Everybody turns in the first homework! You are going to get in so much—"

"I bet the dog ate it," said a smart-aleck kid.

"Or the cat," I mumbled. I wanted to tell Jake that it wasn't my fault my homework wasn't done. I wanted to tell him I had been looking for George. It would be good to tell a loudmouth. He would tell everybody else. Then they'd all understand how I'm not weird. It's just William's cats.

But the bus pulled up before I had a chance to say anything. On the bus, Jake sat with his friends. I had to sit with a big kid.

At least nobody said anything about my socks.

Chapter 10

I tried to do my homework on the bus. But it was bouncy. All that came out of my pencil was scribbles.

In class, we turned in our papers. Mr. Morgan looked hard at mine.

"Holly?" He turned it upside down. "Looks like Urdu." He handed it back. "Why don't we have a chat at recess?"

When the recess bell rang, I stayed at my desk. I sat very still. Maybe Mr. Morgan will forget about me, I thought. But he looked up and said, "Have a seat by my desk, please. Bring the math homework."

Now I was going to get it. He had been nice for a whole day. But no more.

"Your handwriting yesterday was neat," Mr. Morgan said when I had sat down. "So what's all this?"

"It's because of George," I said.

"George?"

I nodded. "George disappeared."

"Disappeared? Why, Holly I'm so *sorry*. Why didn't you tell me? Your mother must be frantic. Did you call the police?"

"I don't think the police would care," I said.

"I'm sure they would care!" said Mr. Morgan.

"And anyway, we finally found him," I said.

"Oh. Well . . . good, then. Uh . . . and George is . . . your little brother?"

"I don't have a little brother. I only have Mom. And I guess now William. And William's cats, if you count cats. Actually, that's what we were doing: counting cats. That's why I was too busy to do my homework." I had a feeling this was coming out all wrong.

"I'm not sure I understand," Mr. Morgan said.

"That's just the trouble." I was frustrated. "*Nobody* understands. And the more I try to explain, the weirder they think I am."

"Holly." Mr. Morgan smiled. "I don't think you're weird. And I'm sure no one else thinks you're weird. You've only been here one day. Usually, it takes three days before we at Market Street School declare somebody weird."

"Oh." I started calculating. I had until Wednesday to convince them I was normal.

"Holly!" Mr. Morgan's voice startled me. "What?!"

"I was kidding! That was a joke! Now let's start over. Who is George? And what do cats have to do with homework?"

This time I guess I explained better. When I was done, Mr. Morgan said it made sense. "Just this once, I won't mark it late if you turn the homework in tomorrow," he said. "Anyway, I don't expect this will happen anymore. From now on when George disappears, you'll know where to look."

I began to think Mr. Morgan might be okay, even when no moms were around.

Chapter 11

At lunch, I sat with Jake the loudmouth, Kimmi from the bus yesterday, and Ashley from Copper Table.

In case you're wondering, all the tables in Room 31 have metal names because we are going to study the earth. I guess I am lucky I sit at Gold. I could sit at Antimony, which is hard to spell.

Lunch was going pretty well. Kimmi asked me about my old school. I told her it was perfect. Then Jake wanted to know how come if it was perfect I changed schools. I told him about my mom. And William's tiny apartment. And my dress that looked like an old lady's tablecloth.

I'm not sure he understood the tablecloth part.

I was going to tell them about how I'm not weird. Only William's cats make me *seem* weird. But then I realized Ashley was staring at my feet. I tried to hide them under the bench. But it was too late.

"Hey, Holly—is that the kind of socks they wear at your old school? All gray and wrinkly? They look like rhino skin!"

I bet I turned jelly red. "It's not my fault! It's William's cats! See—"

"Anybody wanna play kickball?" Jake interrupted. He crumpled his lunch bag and threw it in the trash.

"Me!"

"Me!"

"Me!"

Everybody else crumpled their lunch bags, too.

"Come on, Holly," said Ashley. "And try not to trip over your socks."

When I got home that day, Mom was working in her office that used to be a closet.

"Hello, honey!" she called. "There's a snack in the fridge. I just have to finish this monthly."

I don't know what a "monthly" is either. But Mom is always finishing them.

I set my book bag on my desk and went into the kitchen. The snack was chocolate chip cookies and chocolate milk. I put four cookies on a plate on the table. I poured a glass of milk. I put the milk carton back in the refrigerator. When I turned around, Max and Boo were sitting on the table. Max had one of my cookies in his mouth.

"*Scat!*" I stomped and waved. Max jumped down and ran. The cookie was still in his mouth. Boo grabbed another cookie and leaped onto the kitchen counter.

"Give those back! They're mine!"

Boo ignored me and batted his cookie the way cats bat trapped mice. He got bored when the cookie didn't wiggle. So he knocked it on the

floor. Then he climbed into the dish drainer, sat down, and washed his face.

"Bad cat!" I said to Boo. I picked up the cookie and threw it away. Then I went after Max. There were cookie crumbs in the living room. And cookie crumbs in Mom and William's room. And cookie crumbs in the bathroom. But no Max.

"Mo-o-o-om!" I whined.

"What is it?"

"The stupid cats stole my cookies!"

"Don't say 'stupid,' Holly. It isn't nice." Mom met me in the kitchen and nodded at the table. "Anyway, you still have two cookies left."

I wrinkled my nose. "The cats probably *licked* them."

Mom popped the tin open and got out four more for me. Then she picked up one from my plate and ate it herself. "Mmmmm. Yummy." She licked her lips. "Cat spit adds that certain I-don't-know-what."

"Mo-o-o-o-om," I whined. "Gross! Anyway, I bet cookies aren't good for cats. I bet they get sick. I bet the vet has to pump their stomachs. I bet it costs heaps of money."

Mom ignored me and sat down. "How was school today?"

I told her about my math homework. "So don't ask me to count the stupid cats today, okay?"

"'Stupid?'" she repeated.

"I don't want to count 'genius' cats either."

"You're off the hook," she said. "I already did it. George was in the laundry basket. Anyway, Mr. Morgan sounds like he was quite reasonable about the homework. You're lucky."

I didn't feel lucky. I told her how everybody made fun of my rhino socks.

"Yesterday the slide. Today your socks," she said. "If those are your only complaints, I'd say things are going quite well. And, by the way, there are new socks in your drawer."

Nobody understood. Not even my own mother. So I ate the cookies and stomped off to my tiny room to do my homework.

Chapter 12

Boo had left the dish drainer and was asleep on my desk. I sat down. "Shoo, Boo!" I shoved him. He jumped into my lap. I could smell his cookie breath. It was better than fish breath. I let him stay.

When I wasn't trying to write it on a bus, the math was easy. In fifteen minutes, it was done. I decided to call Sylvie and find out how things were at 19th Street Elementary, my old school.

Sylvie lived in a regular-size house with her own mom and her own dad, her twin teenage brothers, and a smelly dog as big as a pony. His name was Clyde. Sylvie's room was gigantic. Since kindergarten, she had had her own phone number.

Sylvie had the perfect life.

"Holly, I miss you so much!" she said. "School is terrible! My teacher is a witch! Did you know I got Ms. Burke? The spelling words are killing me! Did you know I sit at the same table with Stuart Biggs? He never stops talking, but I'm the one who gets in trouble. Holly—are you still there?"

"I miss you, too," I said.

"So, are the kids nice? Do you have friends? Is your teacher a witch? Did she give homework the first day? How are the cats? I wish I could

have a cat—even only one cat. Holly—are you still there?"

I smiled. Sylvie was so funny. That was why we had been friends since we were babies. She was funny. And I wasn't. We were a good match.

"I'm still here." I tried to remember her questions. "The kids are normal. I don't have friends. My teacher is a man. And I don't think men can be witches." I looked down at Boo. He was asleep. "The cats are stupid and annoying, like always."

"I think you are *so* lucky," Sylvie said. "Cats are cuddly. Can you imagine Clyde in my lap? He'd squish me!"

I sighed. "You don't get it, Syl. The cats wake me up. They eat my socks. They make me late for school. They make me forget my homework. Today they even stole my cookies!"

Sylvie laughed. "You're so funny, Holly!"

"I'm not funny!" My voice caught. I was afraid I might cry. So I took a deep breath. "I'm *terrible*," I said. "I hate living here. I hate William's cats." The phone was silent. "Sylvie?" I said after a minute. "Are you still there?"

"I didn't know it was that bad," she said.

"Could you come over this weekend?"

"I can't. We're going up the coast for a wedding. Outside. Dad says the bride's dress is orange. That way we can see it through the fog. I think he's kidding."

"Could you come next weekend?"

"Okay. I have to ask, though."

"I'll call you," we both said at the same time.

Talking to Sylvie made me feel better. Besides Mr. Morgan, she was the first person who had listened.

Chapter 13

That night we ate a normal dinner: Greek salad with wonton soup and nachos.

Before bed, William offered to read me a book. He was trying to be nice. I let him. We sat on the sofa by the bookshelves. Wilbur Cat was above us, napping on the Oxford English Dictionary.

The book William read to me was about a dog. William did an excellent dog imitation. "Arf! Arf!" he barked.

I laughed, but Wilbur Cat didn't think it was funny. He woke up and swished his tail. I guess William didn't see.

"Arf! Arf!" William barked again.

Wilbur hissed.

"Arf! Arf!"

Wilbur growled.

"Arf! Arf!"

Wilbur leaped—right onto William's bald head!

Everything went wild. William, Mom, and I hollered: "Bad cat!" and "Get down!" Boo and Max *mr-r-r-r-rowed* and jumped: chair-to-sofa, sofa-to-stereo, stereo-to-chair, and round and round.

George, as usual, was nowhere to be seen.

The noise scared Wilbur, and he dug in his claws. William jumped up from the sofa yelling "Owieeeee!"

I picked up the *New Yorker* magazine and tried to swat Wilbur off William's head. Then Wilbur reached out his claws and scratched me. That was his big mistake. He lost his balance and fell to the floor—*thump*. Then he leaped away toward my room.

William was standing in the middle of the living room. His hands covered the scratches. I couldn't see if there was blood. "Oh, my head . . . my head," he moaned. "I'll never think again."

"Come on," said Mom. "We'll get you a Band-Aid. Holly, did he get you, too?"

I looked at my hand. Only a little blood. It hardly counted.

"I'm okay, Mom."

But Mom waved at me to come, too. "You'll need a good wash and a Band-Aid. Cat scratches are nothing to fool with."

Mom took William's arm and steered toward the bathroom.

"What do you suppose got into Wilbur Cat?" William asked her.

"Brain disorder," said Mom. "He thought you were a sock."

Chapter 14

The next morning, Mr. Morgan asked us to work on a math problem: Melba bought two ounces of gold. It cost $700 an ounce. She bought two ounces of silver. It cost $100 an ounce. How much more did Melba spend for gold than silver?

I wanted to know why anyone would name a kid Melba. I wanted to know where Melba got all that money. But anybody knows those questions don't get answered in math. "To solve the problem, we will use teamwork," Mr. Morgan announced.

Mr. Morgan was big on teamwork. Teamwork, he had told us, would teach us to cooperate. Teamwork would help us get to know one another. Teamwork would give each one of us a chance to teach and to learn.

But Mr. Morgan hadn't counted on Zach the know-it-all. Here's what happened on our team: Jake read the problem. We all looked at Zach. Zach said $1,200. I wrote it down.

End of teamwork.

It was Wednesday. The third day of school. Mr. Morgan had told me he was kidding. But I still thought it might be my last day to convince people I wasn't weird. So far, I had failed.

"How come you've got that Band-Aid on your hand?" Zach asked after he had solved the problem.

Mr. Morgan was busy helping another team. So it looked like now might be my chance to explain. Finally.

"It's all because of William's cats," I began. "Mostly Wilbur."

"'Mostly Wilbur' is a dumb name for a cat," said Jake.

"'Mostly Wilbur' is not his name," I said. "*Plain* Wilbur is his name. Anyway—"

Jake interrupted. "I don't think 'Plain Wilbur' is much better—"

Zach interrupted. "Don't be a moron, Jake. The cat's name is Wilbur."

"Yeah," I said. "Anyway, usually Wilbur always eats socks. But last night, he tried to eat William's head."

"William is a good name for a cat," said Kimmi.

"But William is *not* a cat!" I was getting frustrated. "William is my mom's new husband! He's bald," I added.

"I thought you said William always eats socks," said Kimmi.

"Your mom's new husband eats socks?" said Jake.

Listening to them, I thought I would have to get used to being weird. No matter how I tried, things got mixed up.

"Holly?" Zach looked at me. "Are you saying Wilbur is a cat? And William is a husband? And Wilbur attacked William? Then you got in the middle and got scratched? So now you have a Band-Aid on your hand?"

"Yes. Yes, *exactly*!" At last, somebody understood!

Only now nobody was listening. When Zach explained, it didn't sound interesting. And it didn't explain how it was William's cats that made me weird, instead of me that made me weird.

"But, you guys—" I tried to get everybody's attention back. "It's not *just* the Band-Aid. It's falling asleep in class. And being late the first day.

And writing my homework in Urdu. And rhino-skin socks. And cat spit on my cookies. And—"

"Cat spit? *Gross*," Jessica A. said. Jessica A. sits next to Zach. This was the first thing she had said all week.

Cat spit got everybody interested again. They started asking questions all at once.

"Did you eat the cookies?"

"Who's William?"

"How many cats?"

"Do the cats belong to the old lady?"

"What old lady?" I said.

"You know," said Jake, "the one who has the ugly tablecloth."

I ignored him.

"There's just one thing I don't understand," said Zach.

"What's that?" I asked.

"Which one of the cats is bald?"

Now even the know-it-all was confused. And I was as weird as ever.

Chapter 15

At recess, Kimmi came up to me on the playground.

"How many cats do you have, really?" she asked.

I almost didn't bother to answer. Something was going to interrupt. A kid. A teacher. An earthquake.

"Holly?" said Kimmi. "Are you in there?"

"Four." I talked fast. "Four cats. They belong to William. He's the bald one. But he's not a cat. He's the one who—"

"—your mother's new husband," Kimmi said. "I know."

"You do?"

"Sure. I have a stepdad, too. Only he raises begonias. I *love* cats. I wish I had one. Begonias are ugly," Kimmi said. "Their leaves aren't even green."

I told her she wouldn't want William's cats. "They're stupid and annoying." I was so busy explaining I didn't notice where Kimmi and I were walking. Until it was too late. We were in line for the dreaded too-tall slide.

"Oh, no." I stepped back.

"What?" asked Kimmi.

I whispered in her ear.

"You're scared?" she said so loud the whole school heard. *"Of a slide?"*

I bet I turned jelly red.

Then, before everybody could start laughing and calling me "baby" and saying I was chicken, I turned around and ran for it.

I hadn't gone far when I heard the *bwee-eee-eeeeet! bwee-eee-eeeeet!* of the yard teacher's whistle. Somebody was in trouble. "You! Hey, kid!" The yard teacher pointed.

At me?!

"Benched!" She waved me toward the fence where the benches were.

What did I do?

"Running on the kindergarten playground."
She wrote something on her clipboard. "You
might have mowed a little guy down! Two minutes. Now, march!"

I didn't even know I was on the kindergarten
playground. Not to mention, I didn't remember
any rule about not running there. But there were
so many rules. . . .

I marched to the bench and sat down. My
whole class was for sure watching.

Two minutes was a long time. It was plenty to
think about the other worst things that had ever

happened to me: When my parents split up. When I had to fly on the airplane by myself. When I had to wear the tablecloth.

Maybe being benched would be the start of something new. I was already weird. Maybe I could become bad. I could steal lunch money. I could cheat at dodgeball. I could copy off other kids' tests.

Being bad might be okay. But being benched was awful.

Chapter 16

None of the kids in Room 31 teased me about being benched.

And Kimmi acted normal on the bus.

But I still didn't tell Mom when she asked about my day. She didn't understand anything lately. And anyway, I was too embarrassed.

Mom had a meeting after dinner. So I had to stay home with William. He read me a story. It had no dogs in it. So we were safe from cats.

William's bald head had two Band-Aids on it. He looked silly. I wondered if the other lawyers asked him about the Band-Aids. I wondered if he told them his own cat attacked his head. I wondered if he was embarrassed.

After William finished reading, he said, "I feel inspired, Holly. I think I'll put in some time at the keyboard."

He meant he was going to write a story. It would have long words and make no sense.

I walked into my room to get ready for bed. As soon as I was through the door, I smelled it. Something bad. It didn't take long to see what. A little damp, white clump of hairy, gross-out goop.

It was right in the middle of my pillow. Like a present especially for me.

"William!" I skidded into his and Mom's room. He was already working at his computer. "Your stupid cats threw up!"

He swiveled his chair toward me. "All four of them?"

"How do *I* know how many? It's all over my pillow!"

William touched his Band-Aids and sighed. "Another peril of cat ownership." He swiveled back. "There are rags under the sink. A clean pillowcase is in the linen closet."

At first, I didn't get it. Then my mouth dropped open. He expected *me* to clean up cat barf! For a second, I stood there. Then all the mad in me bubbled up.

"I will *not* clean it up!" I said. "They're *your* stupid cats!"

William typed more letters then stopped. The room seemed very quiet. I thought: I am really going to get it now.

Then William said, "Young lady, I am a very patient man. I love your mother. I am willing to love you, too. But I will not tolerate insults—to me, or my cats."

He swiveled around and looked at me. "In my house, we have a rule," he went on. "Perhaps I neglected to mention it. The rule goes like this: He who finds the cat mess, cleans the cat mess. It also applies to a 'she.' Do I make myself clear?"

William kept looking at me. He was waiting for an answer. I stepped back and bumped the bookcase. I felt trapped.

So, for the second time in one day, I turned around and ran for it.

Chapter 17

"Holly?" William's voice followed me to the apartment door. *"Hol—"* I slammed the door.

My high-tops' *squish-squish-squish-squisha* echoed in the stairwell. Any second, I expected to hear footsteps. Or maybe *bwee-ee-eet!*—a whistle like the yard teacher's.

But there was only *squish-squish-squish-squisha*. On the second-to-bottom step, I wondered where I was going. I didn't know anyone in the neighborhood. Sylvie's house was too far. And anyway, I wasn't sure how to get there.

I pushed through the street door onto the sidewalk. It was cold and damp. I didn't have a jacket. I looked at the sky. No stars. The moon was a glow in the fog.

I guess that's what made me think of it: Moon Glow Dough and Joe. I was scared to be out at night by myself. And I was cold. So I ran the whole way down the block. What a relief to see the OPEN sign.

I pushed the door hard and almost fell inside. It was warm and bright. Only three doughnuts on the rack. No customers. The girl who lived in 1-C was cleaning the counter.

"Hey, the kid from my building." She smiled. "Looking for a bedtime snack? We got maple. We got plain. Otherwise, finito till 3 A.M. That's when the baker comes in. Or maybe you want coffee? Kids today, you never can tell."

"Uh . . . I don't have money. . . ." I mumbled. Would she make me leave?

"So you're looking for a freebie?"

I felt myself turn jelly red. I came into a doughnut place. But I didn't have money for a doughnut. How was I supposed to explain that? It made no sense.

"Well, spit it out, kid. Shave and a haircut? Fashion advice? Tattoo?"

I smiled. She was nice, after all. "I just want to be someplace," I said. "I mean, someplace that isn't William's apartment. See, the cat threw up."

She nodded. "Gross-a-matic. Who's William?"

I told her. Then I told her about Mom. Then the cats. Then Market Street School. She cleaned the rest of the counters. When I was done, she said, "I know all about stepfathers. I ran away from mine, too. He used to hit me. I guess William's not like that."

My eyes got big. "No." I shook my head.

"So, soon as I was eighteen, I was gone. It's better. Only it's lonely sometimes. Here." She waved at the three doughnuts. "Which one do you want? Manager lets me take home leftovers." She flipped the OPEN sign to CLOSED. "As of now, it's my gift to you."

"Maple, please."

She got out a paper sack and stuck a maple doughnut in it. "Heck," she said, "I am sick to death of doughnuts." She put in the two plain ones. "Make a peace offering to William and your mom. Don't you think they're worried by now?"

"Oh, gosh!" I had almost forgotten I ran away. "What time is it?"

"Nine o'clock. You've been a missing person for forty-five minutes."

"Oh, gosh! Poor Mom. Maybe she's not home yet. I better go."

"Come on. I'll walk you." She grabbed a coat made of fake cow fur. Then she flipped the light off. Outside, she locked the door with three keys.

"Thanks," I told her as we walked.

"Like I said, I'm sick of doughnuts."

"Not just doughnuts." I waved the paper sack. "You let me stay there. And everything."

"No sweat, sweetcakes. So anyway, what's your name?"

I told her.

"I'm Mary," she said.

"Plain old Mary?" I guess I expected Bluebird or Horizon or Sky Pilot or something.

"Not that plain." She touched her rainbow mohawk. "Not that old." She opened the door. We were in our building. "Want me to come up? I could say I kidnapped you. So you won't get in trouble."

"That's okay," I said. "I think I have to conquer my fear."

Chapter 18

I stopped outside the door to 3-C. I heard voices inside.

"I went to every apartment in the building," William was saying. "No one's seen her. I'm beside myself, darling. I never expected . . ."

"And the police?" Mom's voice was small.

"They're sending an officer. And they have a B.O.L. on her—"

"What's that?" Mom asked.

"Be-on-the-lookout. It means every cop in the city is watching."

"It's not a bit like her," Mom said. "Tell me again, William. What happened?"

Suddenly, I was ashamed of myself. They were

in a panic. Even William. All because I was too mad to clean up cat barf. It didn't make sense to run away for that. It wasn't like a stepdad who hits you.

I pushed open the door. William was hugging Mom on the sofa. The cats were all curled up around them. Mom's face was streaky. She had been crying.

"I'm sorry," I said.

Mom jumped off the sofa. Something rubbed my leg. I looked down in time to see a flash of fur. Max was gone again.

"Oh, honey!" Mom practically knocked me over.

"The cat." My mouth was squished into her body.

"Never mind the *cat*," said William. He hugged us both. "We're so glad to see *you*. We were so worried!"

Mom let go a little and looked into my face. I saw how red her eyes were. I felt even more terrible. "I'm sorry," I said again. "Uh . . . I brought doughnuts." I held up the sack.

"Is *that* where you were? I should have thought—" William said.

"Don't you ever, ever, ever, ever, *ever*—" Mom started. But the doorbell interrupted.

"Oh, dear," said William. He opened the door.
And there stood a policeman. He was clutching a
very squirmy Max.

The policeman nodded at me. "The missing
person?"

"She *was*, yes. She just now came back," Mom
said.

"What about this?" The policeman held out
Max. "Missing this one, too?"

"Thank you." William grabbed him. "*Bad* cat."

"All right, then," said the policeman. "All's well that ends well. As for *you*, young lady. You know what Mark Twain said, don't you?"

I didn't see what it had to do with anything. But I told him: "'The coldest winter I ever spent was a summer in San Francisco'?"

"Nah—that isn't it." The policeman shook his head. "He said, and I quote, 'There's no place like home.'"

Chapter 19

"Nice fellow, that policeman," William said. It was Saturday morning, a week and a day later. Sylvie had spent the night. Now William was walking us to Moon Glow Dough and Joe for breakfast.

"But he was wrong about the quotation," William went on. "Mark Twain never said that."

"Who did, then?" Sylvie asked. I had already told her the story of how I ran away. I felt embarrassed telling her. But friends need to know the stupid things you do. It's one of the jobs of friends.

William opened the door and waved us inside. "I believe it was Shakespeare," he said.

"No way," I said.

"Who then?" William asked.

"Dorothy," I said, "in *The Wizard of Oz*."

"So it was," said William. "And a wise young woman she was. Now then, ladies. I'll return in half an hour. See that you behave yourselves. Agreed?"

We nodded. He gave me five dollars. "Live it up," he said.

We ordered from Mary. "Dough for you." She handed me two maple doughnuts. "And joe for you." She handed Sylvie a cup of coffee. "You know," she whispered to Sylvie, "it will stunt your growth."

Sylvie whispered back, "I put in lots of milk and sugar."

We were sitting at a table when Kimmi's mom dropped her off. "Sorry I'm late," she said. "I had to water begonias."

Everything is getting better. I'm not sure why. Maybe because of William's cats. Or maybe because I started paying attention.

Paying attention happened when Mary told me her stepfather hit her. It was the first time in a while I had listened to anybody except me.

So I hadn't heard Kimmi being friendly. Or Sylvie hating school. Or Mom being extra nice.

And I hadn't even noticed that Boo Cat, at least, likes me. It makes sense. Why else would he always be on my pillow? And in my lap? And in the way?

Speaking of cats: The day after I ran away, Kimmi asked if she could visit sometime. She wanted to meet the cats. Then Jake the loud-mouth and Zach the know-it-all said they wanted to meet the cats, too.

They all came over last Saturday. At first, Zach was disappointed none of the cats was bald. But he got over it.

We had fun.

We caught Max trying to escape.

We played "seek" while George played "hide." (He was under the sink.)

We shared popcorn with Boo. He knocked the bowl over. Then Wilbur chased kernels around the floor. He didn't eat any, though. I guess he still likes socks.

Sylvie called Sunday when she got home from the foggy wedding. It turns out the bride wore red. You could see it through the fog like Rudolph's nose.

I told her, "Guess what? I think now I have friends."

This morning, sun shines through the windows at Moon Glow Dough and Joe. If it stays nice, William is taking us to this park on a hill. It has a really huge slide. Kimmi says the view from the top is great: skyscrapers, fancy old houses, and two swoopy bridges over the sparkling water.

I don't know if I've conquered my fear yet. I don't know if I can slide down such a really huge slide. But I know I can climb up. I'm going to see that view.

Afterwards, I'll go home to my tiny room and our four cats. They're not just William's anymore. They're mine and Mom's, too. I guess we've all learned to share.